Orange Juice

Betsey Chessen • **Pamela Chanko**

Scholastic Inc.

New York • Toronto • London • Auckland • Sydney

Acknowledgments

Science Consultants: Patrick R. Thomas, Ph.D., Bronx Zoo/Wildlife Conservation Park; Glenn Phillips, The New York Botanical Garden; **Literacy Specialist:** Maria Utefsky, Reading Recovery Coordinator, District 2, New York City

Design: MKR Design, Inc.

Photo Research: Barbara Scott

Endnotes: Susan Russell

———————————————

Photographs: Cover: Sandy Clark/The Stock Market; p.1: Ross M. Horowitz/The Image Bank; P. 2: C. Hammell/The Stock Market; p. 3: Wulf Maehl/ ZefA/The Stock Market; p. 4: Robert Brenner/Photo Edit; p. 5: Joe Cornish/Tony Stone Images; p. 6: Timothy O'Keefe/Bruce Coleman Inc.; p. 7: M. Sroka/Third Coast Stock Source; p. 8: Yellow Dog Prods/Image Bank; p. 9: Jim Steinberg/ Photo Researchers, Inc.; p. 10: Ariel Skelley/The Stock Market; p. 11: John Callahan/Tony Stone Images; p. 12: Ariel Skelley/The Stock Market.

Library of Congress Cataloging-in-Publication Data
Chessen, Betsey, 1970-
Orange juice / Betsey Chessen, Pamela Chanko.
p.cm. -- (Science emergent readers)
"Scholastic early childhood."
Includes index.
Summary: Photographs and simple text explain where orange juice comes from, with emphasis on the life cycle of the orange tree.
ISBN 0-590-14999-7 (paperback.: alk. paper)
1. Oranges--Juvenile literature.   2. Orange juice--Juvenile literature
[1. Oranges. 2. Orange juice.]
I. Chanko, Pamela, 1968-   . II. Title. III. Series.
SB307.07C48 1998

634 .31--DC21

97-34206
CIP AC

Orange juice comes from oranges.

From seedlings

to trees.

From flowers

to fruit.

And from harvest

to you!

Orange Juice

Trees are very important to our life here on earth. They create much of the oxygen that we breathe. They give us the wood that we use for building houses and the nuts, fruits, and berries that we eat. Trees are also an important source of food for animals, birds, and insects. The trees that produce fruit are called broadleaved trees. Most of them have wide, flat leaves that are very different from the needles of the conifers. Most of them shed their leaves in winter and are called deciduous because of that. All of the broadleaved trees have flowers that bloom in the spring. The flowers then produce seeds that are held inside a hard nut or a soft fruit. Every tree begins from one of these little seeds that germinate when the earth warms up in early spring.

When the seedling starts to grow it breaks open the seed case, sending a little root down into the ground. The root gathers water and nutrients from the soil and anchors the tiny tree. The seedling then begins to grow up and down at the same time. It sends the main root farther down into the soil and lifts the seed case off the ground, growing upward on its new stem. Leaves develop inside the case, growing, unfolding, and then throwing the case off. The first leaves, called seed leaves, reach for the sunlight and begin to power the growth of the seedling. It then gets its first true leaves and extends its roots. The next season it will have a barklike stem and be a real, though tiny, tree.

Open any piece of fruit and you will find the seeds that can create a new plant. Every season, trees go through the cycle of flower, fruit, seed, and new life. It is the tree's job to reproduce. When birds eat the fruit or berries that contain the seeds, they are helping the tree, although they don't know it. Birds carry the seeds to new locations and deposit them far and wide in their droppings. These seeds will produce new trees. If the seeds fell only under the tree, they probably wouldn't be able to get enough sunlight to grow properly.

Trees must mature before they can reproduce. Fruit trees begin to bloom and produce fruit when they are 6-7 years old. Their fruit nourishes people as well as animals and birds. Fruit trees have been cultivated for many centuries. The ancient Romans planted apple trees. Orange trees originally came from Asia. Carefully selecting seeds from the most promising trees has allowed gardeners to grow fruit that is larger and sweeter than the fruit that grows in the wild.

The trees that grow citrus fruit like lemons, limes, and oranges must be grown in warm climates. Temperatures that dip below freezing can damage the fruit, and the trees as well. Farms that specialize in growing fruit are called orchards. They plant and cultivate many, many trees at once. When the fruit is ripe, it is harvested. Some is selected to go to the grocery stores where we can buy it whole. Some fruit is made into the juice we drink. It takes several oranges to make just one glass of orange juice.